Marriage in Free Society

by Edward Carpenter

Copyright © 2/11/2016
Jefferson Publication

ISBN-13: 978-1530006953

Printed in the United States of America

All rights reserved. No part of this book may be reprinted or reproduced or utilized in any form or by any electronic, mechanical, or other means, now known or hereafter invented, including photocopying and recording, or in any form of storage or retrieval system, without prior permission in writing from the publisher.'

MARRIAGE

OF the great mystery of human Love, and that most intimate personal relation of two souls to each other—perhaps the firmest, most basic and indissoluble fact (after our own existence) that we know; of that strange sense—often, perhaps generally, instantaneous—of long precedent familiarity and kinship, that deep reliance on and acceptation of another in his or her entirety; of the tremendous strength of the chain which thus at times will bind two hearts in lifelong dedication and devotion, persuading and indeed not seldom compelling the persons concerned to the sacrifice of some of the other elements of their lives and characters; and, withal, of a certain inscrutable veiledness from each other which so frequently accompanies the relation of the opposite sexes, and which forms at once the abiding charm, and the pain—sometimes the tragedy—of their union; of this palpitating winged living thing, which one may perhaps call the real Marriage—I would say but little; for indeed it is only fitting or possible to speak of it by indirect language and suggestion, nor may one venture to rudely drag it from its sanctuary into the light of the common gaze.

Compared with this, the actual marriage, in its squalid perversity as we too often have occasion of knowing it, is as the wretched idol of the savage to the reality which it is supposed to represent; and one seems to hear the Aristophanic laughter of the gods as they contemplate man's little clay image of the Heavenly Love—which, cracked in the fire of daily life, he is fain to bind together with rusty hoops of law, and parchment bands, lest it should crumble and fall to pieces altogether.

The whole subject, wide as life itself—as Heaven and Hell—eludes anything like adequate treatment, and we need make no apology for narrowing down our considerations here to just a few practical points; and if we cannot navigate upward into the very heart of the matter—namely, into the causes which make some people love each other with a true and perfect love, and others unite in obedience to but a counterfeit passion—yet we may fairly, I imagine, and with profit, study some of the conditions which give to actual marriage its present form, or which in the future are likely to provide real affection with a more satisfactory expression than it has as a rule to-day.

Yet the subject, even so limited, is one on which it is extremely difficult to get a calm audience. Marriage customs (however much they may differ from race to race) are at any one time and among any one folk remarkably tenacious, being sanctioned by almost a violence of public opinion; and as in the case of theology or politics, their mere discussion is liable to infuriate people— perhaps from the very fact that the subject is so complex and so deeply rooted in personal feeling. Nevertheless—since alterations have to take place in these as in other customs, and since, as many things indicate, we are moving towards a distinct period of change in matters matrimonial—it would seem that the more rationally we can survey these questions beforehand, the better.

It will probably be felt that certain present difficulties in the marriage-relation are not merely casual or local, but are deeply intertwined with a long series of historical causes, which have led up to that exaggerated differentiation, and consequent misunderstanding, between the sexes, of which we have spoken in a former paper.* Behind the relation of any individual man and woman to each other stands the historical age-evolved relation of the two sexes generally, spreading round and enclosing the former on all sides, and creating the social environment from which the individuals can hardly escape. Two young people in the present day may come together, but their relation is already largely determined by causes over which they have no control.

* Woman: Labour Press Society, Manchester.

As a rule they know but little of each other; society has kept the two sexes apart; the boy and the girl have been brought up along different lines; they hardly understand each other's nature; their mental interests and occupations are different; and as they grow up their worldly interests and advantage are seen to be different, often opposed; public opinion separates their spheres and their rights and their duties, and their honor and their dishonor* very sharply from each other. The subject of sex is a sealed book to the girl; to the youth it is possibly a book whose most dismal page has been opened first; in either case with its very mention is probably connected a painful and irrational sense of wickedness.

In this state of confusion of mind, of mutual misunderstanding, and often of suffering, the Sex-glamor suddenly descends upon the two individuals and drives them into each other's arms. It envelopes in a gracious and misty halo all their differences and misapprehensions. They marry without misgiving; and their hearts overflow with gratitude to the white-surpliced old gentleman who reads the service over them. It is only at a later hour, and with calmer thought, that they realise that it is a life-sentence which he has so suavely passed upon them—not reducible (as in the case of ordinary convicts) even to a term of 20 years.

```
    * See Webster's Dictionary, which gives as one
of the
      meanings of Honor, "any particular virtue much
valued, as
      bravery in men and chastity in females."
```

The married life, in so strange and casual a way begun, or drifted into, is hardly, one might think, likely to turn out well. Sometimes, of course, it does; but in many cases, perhaps the majority, there follows a painful awakening. A brief burst of satisfaction, accompanied, probably through sheer ignorance, by gross neglect of the law of transmutation; satiety on the physical plane, followed by vacuity of affection on the higher planes, and that succeeded by boredom, and even nausea; the girl, full perhaps of a tender emotion, and missing the sympathy and consolation she expected in the man's love, only to find its more materialistic side—"This, this then is what I am wanted for." The man, who looked for a companion, finding he can rouse no mortal interest in his wife's mind save in the most exasperating trivialities;—whatever the cause may be, a veil has fallen from before their faces, and there they sit, held together now by the least honorable interests, the interests which they themselves can least respect, but to which Law and Religion lend all their weight. The monetary dependence of the woman, the mere sex-needs of the man, the fear of public opinion, all form motives, and motives of the meanest kind, for maintaining the seeming tie; and the relation of the two hardens down into a dull neutrality, in which lives and characters are narrowed and blunted, and deceit becomes the common weapon which guards divided interests.

A sad picture! and of course in this case a portrayal deliberately of the seamy side of the matter. But who shall make light of the agonies often gone through in those first few years of married life?

It may be said—and often of course is said—that such cases as these only prove that marriage was entered into under the influence of a passing glamor and delusion, and that there was not much real devotion to begin with. And no doubt there is truth enough in such remarks. But—we may say in reply—because two young people make a mistake in youth, to condemn them, for that reason, to lifelong suffering and mutual degradation, or to see them so condemned, without proposing any hope or way of deliverance, but with the one word "serves you right" on the lips, is a course which can commend itself only to the grimmest and dullest Calvinist. Whatever safe-guards against a too frivolous view of the relationship may be proposed by the good sense of society in the future, it is certain that the time has gone past when Marriage can continue to be regarded as a supernatural institution to whose maintenance human bodies and souls must be indiscriminately sacrificed; a humaner, wiser, and less panic-stricken treatment of the subject must set in; and if there are difficulties in the way they must be met by patient and calm consideration of human welfare— superior to any law, however ancient and respectable.

I take it then that, without disguising the fact that the question is a complex one, and that our conclusions may be only very tentative, we have to consider as rationally as we conveniently can, first, some of the drawbacks or defects of the present marriage-customs, and secondly such improvements in these as may suggest themselves to us, and as may seem feasible.

And if we turn to the question of how things stand in the present day, one of the first points to strike us—and one that we have already touched on in another paper*—is the serious want of any special teaching to young folk on matters of love and sex, and the responsibility resting on parents and teachers to supply this want. That one ought to distinguish a passing sex-spell from a true comradeship and devotion is no doubt a wise remark, but that it is often difficult, even for adults, to do so makes it all the more necessary that young people should have some rational ideas on the subject, and above all that they should get some understanding of the nature of that true love which alone can make marriage a success. The search for a fitting mate, especially among the more sensitive and highly-organised types of mankind, is a most complex affair. And it is indeed hard that the young man or woman should have to set out—as they mostly have to do to-day—on this difficult quest without a word of suggestion or help, as to the choice of the way or the very real perplexites and doubts that beset it.

```
   *Sex-Love, and its place in a Free Society.
Labour Press,
    Manchester.
```

Then, besides this more general teaching, it is also highly necessary that those in question should have some knowledge of the use and guardianship of their own sex-functions. If the youth and girl whom we have supposed as about to be married had been brought up in almost any tribe of savages, they would a few years previously have gone through regular offices of initiation into manhood and womanhood, during which time ceremonies (possibly indecent in our eyes) would at any rate have made many misapprehensions impossible. As it is, the civilised girl is led to the 'altar;' often in uttermost ignorance and misunderstanding as to the nature of the sacrificial rites about to be consummated. The youth too (does it not seem strange?) has never been taught how to use the female in this most important moment of their joint lives. Perhaps he is unaware that love in the female is, in a sense, more diffused than in the male, less specially sexual; that it dwells longer in caresses and embraces, and determines itself more slowly towards the reproductive system. Impatient, he injures and horrifies his partner, and unconsciously perhaps aggravates the very hysterical tendency which marriage might and should have allayed.*

Among the middle and well-to-do classes especially, the conditions of high civilisation, by inducing an overfed masculinity in the males and a nervous and hysterical tendency in the females,** increase the difficulties mentioned; and it is among the 'classes' too that public opinion, largely by repressing the utterance and ignoring the existence of sex-feeling, has created the special evils of sex-starvation and sex-ignorance on the one hand, and of mere licentiousness on the other.

> * It must be remembered too that to many women (though of
> course by no means a majority) the thought of Sex brings
> little sense of pleasure, and the fulfilment of its duties
> constitutes a real, even though a willing, sacrifice.
>
> ** Thus Bebel in his book on Woman speaks of "the idle and
> luxuriant life of so many women in the upper classes, the
> nervous stimulant afforded by exquisite perfumes, the over-
> dosing with poetry, music, the stage—which is regarded as
> the chief means of education, and is the chief occupation,
> of a sex already suffering from hypertrophy of nerves and
> sensibility."

Among the comparatively uncivilised mass of the people, where a good deal of familiarity between the sexes exists before marriage, and where indeed marriage not unfrequently follows on sex-connection, these special evils are not so prominent. But among the masses the crying need for some sensible and coherent teaching for the young is only too clear; and it is perhaps among the masses that the neglect of the law of transmutation works to more evil results than among the classes; since among the former—sex-intercourse being comparatively accessible, and obstacles to marriage (from monetary and other considerations) comparatively infrequent—the feeling is liable to flow far too much along the mere physical channels; and the romance and sweet comradeship of love, especially after marriage, comes too often to be replaced by an inert and indeed rather brutish sentiment of simple juxtaposition.

So far with regard to difficulties arising from personal ignorance or inexperience in youth. But stretching beyond and around all these are those other difficulties which are due to the marked special relation of the woman to the man in civilised society generally, and of the man to the woman; and which arise from deep-lying historic and economic causes. Into the large subject of these causes it is not necessary to enter here. Suffice it to say that the difference in physical strength between the sexes, together with woman's disability during the period of child-birth and rearing, gave man from early times an advantage, which complicating itself during the historical period has ultimated (though not of course in the present day only) in what may be called the slavery of woman, her subordination to man, and dependence on him for the means of subsistence; the result being that, till a comparatively few years ago, the woman was condemned to the most special and indeed narrow sphere of life and action; her education, as for this sphere, was most limited, and quite different from that of the man; and her interests were wholly diverse from and often quite opposed to his. Under these circumstances there was naturally little common ground for Marriage, *except* sex. And the same remains largely true even down to to-day. The sex-needs once satisfied, and the emotional charm weakened or undone, man and wife not unfrequently wake up with something like dismay to find how little they have left in common; to find that they have nothing in which they can take interest together; that they cannot work at the same things, that they cannot read the same books, that they cannot keep up half-an-hour's conversation together on any topic, and that secretly they are cherishing their own thoughts and projects quite apart from each other.

It must suffice too to remind the reader quite briefly that this divergence has crept deep down into the moral and intellectual natures of the two sexes, exaggerating the naturally complementary relation of the male and female into a painful caricature of strength on the one hand and dependence on the other. This is well seen in the ordinary marriage-relation of the common-prayer-book type. The frail and delicate female is supposed to cling round the sturdy husband's form, or to depend from his arm in graceful incapacity; and the spectator is called upon to admire the charming effect of the union—as of the ivy with the oak—forgetful of the terrible moral, namely, that (in the case of the trees at any rate) it is really a death-struggle which is going on, in which either the oak must perish suffocated in the embraces of its partner, or in order to free the former into anything like healthy development the ivy must be sacrificed.

Too often of course of such marriages the egoism, lordship and physical satisfaction of the man are the chief motive causes. The woman is practically sacrificed to the part of the maintenance of these male virtues. It is for her to spend her days in little forgotten details of labor and anxiety for the sake of the man's superior comfort and importance, to give up her needs to his whims, to 'humour' him in all ways she can; it is for her to wipe her mind clear of all opinions in order that she may hold it up as a kind of mirror in which he may behold reflected his lordly self; and it is for her to sacrifice even her physical health and natural instincts in deference to what is called her 'duty' to her husband.

How bitterly *alone* many such a woman feels! She has dreamed of being folded in the arms of a strong man, and surrendering herself, her life, her mind, her all, to his service. Of course it is an unhealthy dream, an illusion, a mere luxury of love; and it is destined to be dashed. She has to learn that self-surrender may be just as great a crime as self-assertion. She finds that her very willingness to be sacrificed only fosters in the man, perhaps for his own self-defence, the egotism and coldness that so cruelly wound her.

For how often does he with keen prevision see that if he gives way from his coldness the clinging dependent creature will infallibly overgrow and smother him!—that she will cut her woman-friends, will throw aside all her own interests and pursuits in order to 'devote' herself to him, and, affording no sturdy character of her own in which *he* can take any interest, will hang the festoons of her affection on every ramification of his wretched life—nor leave him a corner free—till he perishes from all manhood and social or heroic uses into a mere matrimonial clothespeg, a warning and a wonderment to passers by!

However, as a third alternative, it sometimes happens that the Woman, too wise to sacrifice her own life indiscriminately to the egoism of her husband, and not caring for the 'festoon' method, adopts the middle course of *appearing* to minister to him while really pursuing her own purposes. She cultivates the gentle science of indirectness. While holding up a mirror for the Man to admire himself in, *behind that mirror* she goes her own way and carries out her own designs, separate from him; and while sacrificing her body to his wants, she does so quite deliberately and for a definite reason, namely, because she has found out that she can so get a shelter for herself and her children, and can solve the problem of that maintenance which society has hitherto denied to her in her own right. For indeed by a cruel fate women have been placed in exactly that position where the sacrifice of their self-respect for base motives has easily passed beyond a temptation into being a necessity. They have had to live, and have too often only been able to do so by selling themselves into bondage to the man. Willing or unwilling, overworked or dying, they have had to bear children to the caprice of their lords; and in this serf-life their very natures have been blunted; they have lost—what indeed should be the very glory and crown of woman's being—the perfect freedom and the purity of their love.

At this whole spectacle of woman's degradation the human male has looked on with stupid and open-mouthed indifference—as an ox might look on at a drowning oxherd—not even dimly divining that his own fate was somehow involved. He has calmly and obliviously watched the woman drift farther and farther away from him, till at last, with the loss of an intelligent and mutual understanding between the sexes, Love with unequal wings has fallen lamed to the ground. Yet it would be idle to deny that even in such a state of affairs as that depicted, men and women have in the past and do often even now find some degree of satisfaction—simply indeed because their types of character are such as belong to, and have been evolved in accordance with, this relation.

To-day, however, there are thousands of women—and everyday more thousands—to whom such a lopsided alliance is detestable; who are determined that they will no longer endure the arrogant lordship and egoism of men, nor countenance in themselves or other women the craft and servility which are the necessary complements of the relation; who see too clearly in the oak-and-ivy marriage its parasitism on the one hand and strangulation on the other to be sensible of any picturesqueness; who feel too that they have capacities and powers of their own which need space and liberty, and some degree of sympathy and help, for their unfolding; and who believe that they have work to do in the world, as important in its own way as any that men do in theirs. Such women have broken into open warfare—not against marriage, but against a marriage which makes true and equal love an impossibility. They feel that as long as women are economically dependent they *cannot* stand up for themselves and insist on those rights which men from stupidity and selfishness will not voluntarily grant them.

On the other hand there are thousands—and one would hope every day more thousands—of men who (whatever their forerunners may have thought) do *not* desire or think it delightful to have a glass continually held up for them to admire themselves in; who look for a partner in whose life and pursuits they can find some interest, rather than for one who has no interest but in them; who think perhaps that they would rather minister than be (like a monkey fed with nuts in a cage) the melancholy object of another person's ministrations; and who at any rate feel that love, in order to be love at all, must be absolutely open and sincere, and free from any sentiment of dependence or inequality. They see that the present cramped condition of women is not only the cause of the false relation between the sexes, but that it is the fruitful source—through its debarment of any common interests—of that fatal boredom of which we have spoken, and which is the bugbear of marriage; and they would gladly surrender all of that masterhood and authority which is supposed to be their due, if they could only get in return something like a frank and level comradeship.

Thus while we see in the present inequality of the sexes an undoubted source of marriage troubles and unsatisfactory alliances, we see also forces at work which are tending to reaction, and to bringing the two nearer again to each other—so that while differentiated they will not perhaps in the future be quite so *much* differentiated as now, but only to a degree which will enhance and adorn, instead of destroy, their sense of mutual sympathy.

There is another point which ought to be considered as contributing to the ill-success of many marriages, and which no doubt is closely connected with that just discussed—but which deserves separate treatment. I mean the harshness of the line which social opinion (at any rate in this country) draws round the married pair with respect to their relations to outsiders. On the one hand, and within the matrimonial relation, society allows practically the utmost passional excess or indulgence, and condones it; on the other hand (I am speaking of the middling bulk of the people, not of the extreme aristocratic and slum classes) beyond that limit, the slightest familiarity, or any expression of affection which might by any possibility be interpreted as deriving from sexual feeling, is sternly anathematised.

Marriage, by a kind of absurd fiction, is represented as an oasis situated in the midst of an arid desert—in which latter, it is pretended, neither of the two parties is so fortunate as to find any objects of real affectional interest. If they do they have carefully to conceal the same from the other party.

The result of this convention is obvious enough. The married pair, thus *driven* as well as drawn into closest continual contact with each other, are put through an ordeal which might well cause the stoutest affection to quail. Not only, as already pointed out, have the man and the wife too few joint interests in the great world, few common plans, projects, purposes, 'causes,' recreations; but—by this insistance of public opinion—all outside interests of a *personal* nature, except of the most abstract kind, are also debarred; if there happens to be any natural jealousy in the case it is heightened and made the more imperative; and unless the contracting parties are fortunate enough to be, both of them, of such a temperament that they are capable of strong attachments to persons of their own sex—and this does not always exclude jealousy—they must be condemned to have no intimate friendships of any kind except what they can find at their own fireside.

It is necessary here to point out, not only how dull a place this makes the home, but also how narrowing it acts on the lives of the married pair. However appropriate the union may be in itself it cannot be good that it should degenerate—as it tends to degenerate so often, and where man and wife are most faithful to each other, into a mere *égoisme à deux*. And right enough no doubt as a great number of such unions actually are, it must be confessed that the bourgeois marriage as a rule, and just in its most successful and pious and respectable form, carries with it an odious sense of Stuffiness and narrowness, moral and intellectual; and that the type of Family which it provides is too often like that which is disclosed when on turning over a large stone we disturb an insect. Home that seldom sees the light.

But in cases where the marriage does not happen to be particularly successful or unsuccessful, when perhaps a true but not overpoweringly intense affection is satiated at a needlessly early stage by the continual and unrelieved impingement of the two personalities on each other, then the boredom resulting is something frightful to contemplate—and all the more so because of the genuine affection behind it, which contemplates with horror its own suicide. The weary couples that may be seen at seaside places and pleasure resorts—the respectable working-man with his wife trailing along by his side, or the highly respectable stock-jobber arm-in-arm with his better and larger half—their blank faces, utter want of any common topic of conversation which has not been exhausted a thousand times already, and their obvious relief when the hour comes which will take them back to their several and divided occupations—these illustrate sufficiently what I mean. The curious thing is that jealousy (accentuated as it is by social opinion) sometimes increases in exact proportion to mutual boredom; and there are thousands of cases of married couples leading a cat-and-dog life, and knowing that they weary each other to distraction, who for that very reason dread all the more to lose sight of each other, and thus never get a chance of that holiday from their own society, and renewal of outside interests, which would make a genuine affectional association possible.

Thus the sharpness of the line which society draws around the pair, and the kind of fatal snap-of-the-lock with which marriage suddenly cuts them off from the world, not only precluding the two, as might fairly be thought advisable, from sexual, but also barring any openly affectional relations with outsiders, and corroborating the selfish sense of monopoly which each has in the other,—these things lead inevitably to the narrowing down of lives and the blunting of general human interests, to intense mutual ennui, and when (as an escape from these evils) outside relations are covertly indulged in, to prolonged and systematic deceit.

From all which the only conclusion seems to be that marriage must be either alive or dead. As a dead thing it can of course be petrified into a hard and fast formula, but if it is to be a living bond, that living bond must be trusted to, to hold the lovers together; nor be too forcibly stiffened and contracted by private jealousy and public censorship, lest the thing that it would preserve for us perish so, and cease altogether to be beautiful. It is the same with this as with everything else. If we would have a living thing, we must give that thing some degree of liberty—even though liberty bring with it risk. If we would debar all liberty and all risk, then we can have only the mummy and dead husk of the thing.

Thus far I have had the somewhat invidious task, but perhaps necessary as a preliminary one, of dwelling on the defects and drawbacks of the present marriage system. I am sensible that, with due discretion, some things might have been said, which have not been said, in its praise; its successful, instead of its unsuccessful, instances might have been cited; and taking for granted the dependence of women, and other points which have already been sufficiently discussed—it might have been possible to show that the bourgeois arrangement was on the whole as satisfactory as could be expected. But such a course would neither have been sincere, nor have served any practical purpose. In view of the actually changing relations between the sexes, it is obvious that changes in the form of the marriage institution are impending, and the questions which are really pressing on folks' mind are: What are those changes going to be; and, Of what kind do we wish them to be?

In answer to the last question it is not improbable that the casual reader might suppose the writer of these pages to be in favor of a general and indiscriminate loosening of all ties—for indeed it is always easy to draw a large inference even from a careful expression.

But such a conclusion would be rash. There is little doubt, I think, that the compulsion of the marriage-tie (whether moral, social, or merely legal) acts beneficially in a considerable number of cases—though it is obvious that the more the compelling force takes a moral or social form and the less purely legal it is, the better; and that any changes which led to a cheap and continual transfer of affections from one object to another would be disastrous both to the character and happiness of a population. While we are bound to see that the marriage-relation—in order to become the indwelling-place of Love—must be made far more *free* than it is at present, we may also recognise that a certain amount of external pressure is not (as things are at least) without its uses: that, for instance, it tends on the whole to concentrate affectional experience and romance on one object, and that though this may mean a loss at times in breadth it means a gain in depth and intensity; that, in many cases, if it were not for some kind of bond, the two parties, after their first passion for each other was past, and when the unavoidable period of friction had set in, might in a moment of irritation easily fly apart, whereas being forced for a while to tolerate each other's defects they learn thereby one of the best lessons of life—a tender forbearance and gentleness, which as time goes on does not unfrequently deepen again into a more pure and perfect love even than at first—a love founded indeed on the first physical intimacy, but concentrated and intensified by years of linked experience, of twined associations, of shared labors, and of mutual forgiveness; and in the third place that the existence of a distinct tie or pledge discredits the easily-current idea that mere pleasure-seeking is to be the object of the association of the sexes—a phantasmal and delusive notion, which if it once got its head, and the bit between its teeth, might soon dash the car of human advance in ruin to the ground.

But having said thus much, it is obvious that external public opinion and pressure are looked upon only as having an *educational* value; and the question arises whether there is beneath this any *reality* of marriage which will ultimately emerge and make itself felt, enabling men and women to order their relations to each other, and to walk freely, unhampered by props or pressures from without.

And it would hardly be worth while writing on this subject, if one did not believe in some such reality. Practically I do not doubt that the more people think about these matters, and the more experience they have, the more they must ever come to feel that there *is* such a thing as a permanent and life-long union—perhaps a many-life-long union—founded on some deep elements of attachment and congruity in character; and the more they must come to prize the constancy and loyalty which rivets such unions, in comparison with the fickle passion which tends to dissipate them.

In all men who have reached a certain grade of evolution, and certainly in almost all women, the deep rousing of the sexual nature carries with it a romance and tender emotional yearning towards the object of affection, which lasts on and is not forgotten, even when the sexual attraction has ceased to be strongly felt. This, in favorable cases, forms the basis of what may almost be called an amalgamated personality. That there should exist one other person in the world towards whom all openness of interchange should establish itself, from whom there should be no concealment; whose body should be as dear to one, in every part, as one's own; with whom there should be no sense of Mine or Thine, in property or possession; into whose mind one's thoughts should naturally flow, as it were to know themselves and to receive a new illumination; and between whom and oneself there should be a spontaneous rebound of sympathy in all the joys and sorrows and experiences of life; such is perhaps one of the dearest wishes of the soul. It is obvious however that this state of affairs cannot be reached at a single leap, but must be the gradual result of years of intertwined memory and affection. For such a union Love must lay the foundation, but patience and gentle consideration and self-control must work unremittingly to perfect the structure. At length each lover comes to know the complexion of the other's mind, the wants, bodily and mental, the needs, the regrets, the satisfactions of the other, almost as his or her own—and without prejudice in favor of self rather than in favor of the other; above all, both parties come to know in course of time, and after perhaps some doubts and trials, that the great want, the great need, which holds them together, is not going to fade away into thin air, but is going to become stronger and more indefeasible as the years go on. There falls a sweet, an irresistible, trust over their relation to each other, which consecrates as it were the double life, making both feel that nothing can now divide; and robbing each of all desire to remain, when death has indeed (or at least in outer semblance) removed the other.*

```
    It is curious that the early Church Service had
"Till
    death us depart"—but in 1661 this was altered to
"Till
    death us do part."
```

So perfect and gracious a union—even if not always realised—is still, I say, the *bonâ fide* desire of most of those who have ever thought about such matters. It obviously yields far more and more enduring joy and satisfaction in life than any number of frivolous relationships. It commends itself to the common sense, so to speak, of the modern mind—and does not require, for its proof, the artificial authority of Church and State. At the same time it is equally evident—and a child could understand this—that it requires some rational forbearance and self-control for its realisation, and it is quite intelligible too, as already said, that there *may* be cases in which a little outside pressure, of social opinion, or even actual law, may be helpful for the supplementing or re-inforcement of the weak personal self-control of those concerned.

The modern Monogamic Marriage however, certified and sanctioned by Church and State, though apparently directed to this ideal, has for the most part fallen short of it. For in constituting—as in a vast number of cases—a union resting on *nothing* but the outside pressure of Church and State, it constituted a thing obviously and by its nature bad and degrading; while in its more successful instances by a too great exclusiveness it has condemned itself to a fatal narrowness and stuffiness.

Looking back to the historical and physiological aspects of the question it might of course be contended—and probably with some truth—that the human male is, by his nature and needs, polygamous. Nor is it necessary to suppose that polygamy in certain countries and races is by any means so degrading or unsuccessful an institution as some folk would have it to be.* But, as Letourneau in his "Evolution of Marriage" points out, the progress of society in the past has on the whole been from confusion to distinction; and we may fairly suppose that with the progress of our own race (for each race no doubt has its special genius in such matters), and as the spiritual and emotional sides of man develop in relation to the physical, there is probably a tendency for our deeper alliances to become more unitary. Though it might be said that the growing complexity of man's nature would be likely to lead him into more rather than fewer relationships, yet on the other hand it is obvious that as the depth and subtlety of any attachment that will really hold him increases, so does such attachment become more permanent and durable, and less likely to be realised in a number of persons. Woman, on the other hand, cannot be said to be by her physical nature polyandrous as man is polygynous. Though of course there are plenty of examples of women living in a state of polyandry both among savage and civilised peoples, yet her more limited sexual needs, and her long periods of gestation, render one mate physically sufficient for her; while her more clinging affectional nature perhaps accentuates her capacity of absorption in the one.

```
    * See R. F. Burton's Pilgrimage to El-Medinah
and Meccah,
        ch. xxiv. He says however "As far as my limited
observations
            go polyandry is the only state of society in
which jealousy
            and quarrels about the sex are the exception and
not the
            rule of life!"
```

In both man and woman then we may say that we find a distinct tendency towards the formation of this double unit of wedded life (I hardly like to use the word Monogamy on account of its sad associations)—and while we do not want to stamp such natural unions with any false irrevocability or dogmatic exclusiveness, what we do want is a recognition to-day of the tendency to their formation as a natural *fact*, independent of any artificial laws, just as one might believe in the natural bias of two atoms of certain different chemical substances to form a permanent compound atom or molecule. Such unions as that depicted a page or two back, built up by patient and loving care over a long stretch of years, and becoming at last in a sense impregnable, do, we maintain, by their actual growth and evolution exemplify this tendency.

It might not be so very difficult to get quite young people to understand this—to understand that even though they might have to contend with some superfluity of passion in early years, yet that the most permanent and most deeply-rooted desire within them will in all probability lead them at last to find their complete happiness and self-fulfilment only in a close union with a life-mate; and that towards this end they must be prepared to use self-control to prevent the aimless straying of their passions, and patience and tenderness towards the realisation of the union when its time comes. Probably most youths and girls, at the age of romance, would easily appreciate this position; and it would bring to them a much more effective and natural idea of the sacredness of Marriage than they ever get from the artificial thunder of the Church and the State on the subject.

No doubt the suggestion of the mere possibility of any added freedom of choice and experience in the relations of the sexes will be very alarming to some people—but it is so, I think, not because they are at all ignorant that men already take to themselves considerable latitude, and that a distinct part of the undoubted evils that accompany that latitude springs from the fact that it is not recognised; not because they are ignorant that a vast number of respectable women and girls suffer frightful calamities and anguish by reason of the utter *inexperience* of sex in which they are brought up and have to live; but because such good people assume that any the least loosening of the formal barriers between the sexes must mean (and must be meant to mean) an utter dissolution of all ties, and the reign of mere licentiousness. They are convinced that nothing but the most unyielding and indeed exasperating straight-jacket can save society from madness and ruin.

To such folk the appearance of our child—the real Marriage—now presented for their consideration (not without some care it must be admitted, as to the smoothing of its hair and pinafore, and the trimming of its naughty little nails) will be strangely disquieting. Accustomed to look on human nature as essentially bad, and on Law and Convention as the *only* things that restrain it from wild excess, it will be hard for them to believe that there is any formative principle of decent life in the apparition before them. We are however prepared to contend that, appearances or prejudices notwithstanding there is a heart of goodness in the young thing; and that, anyhow, whatever we may think or wish, it is here already and among us, and that practically what we have to do is to consider how it can best be made to grow up into a useful member of society.

In fact, and to leave metaphor; when after quietly looking all round the subject we have satisfied ourselves that the formation of a mere or less permanent double unit is—for our race and time—on the whole the natural and ascendant law of sex-union, slowly and with whatever exceptions establishing and enforcing itself independently of any artificial enactments that exist, then we shall not feel called upon to tear our hair or rend our garments at the prospect of added freedom for the operation of this force, but shall rather be anxious to consider how it may best *be* freed and given room for development and growth to its most perfect use in the social order. And it will probably seem to us (looking back to the earlier part of this paper) that the points which most need consideration, as means to this end, are (1) the furtherance of the freedom and self-dependence of women; (2) the provision of some rational teaching, of heart and of head, for both sexes during the period of youth; (3) the recognition in marriage itself of a freer, more companionable, and less pettily exclusive relationship; and (4) the abrogation or modification of the present odious law which binds people together for *life*, without scruple, and in the most artificial and ill-assorted unions.

It must be admitted that the first point (1) is of basic importance. As true Freedom cannot be without Love, so true Love cannot be without Freedom. You cannot truly give yourself to another, unless you are master or mistress of yourself to begin with. Not only has the general *custom* of the self-dependence and self-ownership of women to be gradually introduced, but the Law has to be altered in a variety of cases where it lags behind the public conscience in these matters—as in actual marriage, where it still leaves woman uncertain as to her rights over her own body, or in politics, where it still denies to her a voice in the framing of the laws which are to bind her. And beyond this, since in the modern industrial-commercial State all Freedom has to be largely based on industrial and monetary freedom, it is obviously of paramount necessity that woman should have liberal access to professional spheres and the means of securing her own independent monetary position through ordinary industrial channels. Whatever the future may bring about in the way of a changed social order and a consequently changed basis for woman's independence, it is clear that as things are now, and for a long time yet, her real freedom can only be secured through her command, even in the face of man, of the ordinary resources of the wage-earner.

With regard to (2) hardly any one at this time of day would seriously doubt the desirability of giving adequate teaching to boys and girls. That is a point on which we have sufficiently touched, and which need not be farther discussed here. But beyond this it is important, and especially perhaps, as things stand now, for girls— that each youth or girl should personally see enough of the other sex at an early period to be able to form some kind of judgment of his or her relation to that sex and to sex-matters generally. It is monstrous that the first case of sex-glamor—the true nature of which would be exposed by a little experience—should, perhaps for two people, decide the destinies of a life-time. Yet the more the sexes are kept apart, the more overwhelming does this glamor become, and the more ignorance is there, on either side, as to its nature. No doubt it is one of the great advantages of co-education of the sexes, that it tends to diminish these evils. Co-education, games and sports to some extent in common, and the doing away with the absurd superstition that because Corydon and Phyllis happen to kiss each other sitting on a gate, therefore they must live together all their lives, would soon mend matters considerably. Nor would a reasonable familiarity between the sexes in youth— tempered, as it would be, by previous education and by the subsidence of the blind passion—necessarily mean an increase of casual or clandestine sex-relations. But even if casualties of this kind did occur they would not be the fatal and unpardonable sins that they now at least for girls—are considered to be. Though the recognition of anything like common pre-matrimonial sex-intercourse would probably be foreign to the temper of a northern nation; yet it is open to question whether Society here, in its mortal and fetichistic dread of the thing, has not, by keeping the young of both sexes in ignorance and darkness and seclusion from each other, created worse ills and suffering than it has prevented, and whether it has not indeed intensified the particular evil that it dreaded, rather than abated it.

In the next place (3) we come to the establishment in marriage itself of a freer and broader and more healthy relationship than generally exists at the present time. Attractive as the ideal of the exclusive attachment is, it runs the fatal risk, as we have already pointed out, of lapsing into a mere stagnant double selfishness.

But, in this world, Love is fed not by what it takes, but by what it gives; and the very excellent dual love of man and wife must be fed also by the love they give to others. If they cannot come out of their secluded haven to reach a hand to others, or even to give some boon of affection to those who need it more than themselves, or if they mistrust each other in doing so, then assuredly they are not very well fitted to live together.

A marriage, so free, so spontaneous, that it would allow of wide excursions of the pair from each other, in common or even in separate objects of work and interest, and yet would hold them all the time in the bond of absolute sympathy, would by its very freedom be all the more poignantly attractive, and by its very scope and breadth all the richer and more vital—would be in a sense indestructible; like the relation of two suns which, revolving in fluent and rebounding curves, only recede from each other in order to return again with renewed swiftness into close proximity—and which together blend their rays into the glory of one cosmic double star.

It has been the inability to see or understand this very simple truth that has largely contributed to the failure of the Monogamic union. The narrow physical passion of jealousy, the petty sense of private property in another person, social opinion, and legal enactments, have all converged to choke and suffocate wedded love in egoism, lust, and meanness. But surely it is not very difficult (for those who believe in the real thing) to imagine so sincere and natural a trust between man and wife that neither would be greatly alarmed at the other's friendship with a third person, nor conclude at once that it meant mere infidelity—or difficult even to imagine that such a friendship might be hailed as a gain by both parties. And if it is quite impossible (to some people) to see in such intimacies anything but a confusion of all sex-relations and a chaos of mere animal desire, we can only reply that this view of the situation is probably one that arises greatly out of the present marriage system, and the modes of thought which it engenders—and that anyhow the difficulty to which it refers is likely to be guarded against better by candor and a little common sense than by hysterics and deception. In order to suppose a rational marriage at all one must credit the parties concerned with some modicum of common sense and self-control.

Withal, seeing the remarkable and immense *variety* of love in human nature, when the feeling is really touched—how the love-offering of one person's soul and body is entirely different from that of another person's, so much so as almost to require another name—how one passion is predominantly physical, and another predominantly emotional, and another contemplative, or spiritual, or practical, or sentimental; how in one case it is jealous and exclusive, and in another hospitable and free, and so forth—it seems rash to lay down any very hard and fast general laws for the marriage-relation, or to insist that a real and honorable affection can only exist under this or that special form. It is probably through this fact of the variety of love that it does remain possible, in some cases, for married people to have intimacies with outsiders, and yet to remain perfectly true to each other; and in rare instances, for triune and other such relations to be permanently maintained.

We now come to the last consideration, namely (4) the modification of the present law of marriage. It is pretty clear that people will not much longer consent to pledge themselves irrevocably for life as at present. And indeed there are already plentiful indications of a growing change of practice. The more people come to recognise the sacredness and naturalness of the real union, the less will they be willing to bar themselves from this by a life-long and artificial contract made in their salad days. Hitherto the great bulwark of the existing institution has been the dependence of Women, which has given each woman a direct and most material interest in keeping up the supposed sanctity of the bond—and which has prevented a man of any generosity from proposing an alteration which would have the appearance of freeing himself at the cost of the woman; but as this fact of the dependence of women gradually dissolves out, and as the great fact of the spiritual nature of the true Marriage crystalises into more clearness—so will the formal bonds which bar the formation of the latter gradually break away and become of small import.

Love when felt at all deeply has an element of transcendentalism in it, which makes it the most natural thing in the world for the two lovers—even though drawn together by a passing sex-attraction—to swear eternal troth to each other; but there is something quite diabolical and mephistophelean in the practice of the Law, which creeping up behind, as it were, at this critical moment, and overhearing the two thus pledging themselves, claps its book together with a triumphant bang, and exclaims: "There now you are married and done for, for the rest of your natural lives."

What actual changes in Law and Custom the collective sense of society will bring about is a matter which in its detail we cannot of course foresee or determine. But that the drift will be, and must be, towards greater freedom is pretty clear. Ideally speaking it is plain that anything like a perfect union must have perfect freedom for its condition; and while it is quite supposable that a lover might out of the fulness of his heart make promises and give pledges, it is really almost inconceivable that anyone having that delicate and proud sense which marks deep feeling, could possibly *demand* a promise from his loved one. As there is undoubtedly a certain natural reticence in sex, so perhaps the most decent thing in true Marriage would be to say nothing, make no promises—either for a year or a lifetime. Promises are bad at any time, and when the heart is full silence befits it best. Practically, however, since a love of this kind is slow to be realised, since social custom is slow to change, and since the partial dependence and slavery of Woman must yet for a while continue, it is likely for such period that formal contracts of some kind will still be made; only these (it may be hoped) will lose their irrevocable and rigid character, and become in some degree adapted to the needs of the contracting parties.

Such contracts might of course, if adopted, be very very various in respect to conjugal rights, conditions of termination, division of property, responsibility for and rights over children, etc. In some cases* they might be looked upon as preliminary to a more permanent alliance to be made later on; in others they would provide for disastrous marriages, a remedy free from the inordinate scandals of the present Divorce Courts. It may however be said that rather than adopt any new system of contracts, public opinion in this country would tend to a simple facilitation of Divorce, and that if the latter were made (with due provision for the children) to depend on mutual consent, it would become little more than an affair of registration, and the scandals of the proceeding would be avoided. In any case we think that marriage-contracts, if existing at all, must tend more and more to become matters of private arrangement as far as the relations of husband and wife are concerned, and that this is likely to happen in proportion as woman becomes more free, and therefore more competent to act in her own right. It would be felt intolerable, in any decently constituted society, that the old blunderbuss of the Law should interfere in the delicate relations of wedded life. As it is to-day the situation is most absurd. On the one hand, having been constituted from times back in favor of the male, the Law still gives to the husband barbarous rights over the person of his spouse; on the other hand, to compensate for this, it rushes in with the farcicalities of Breach of Promise; and in any case, having once pronounced its benediction over a pair—however hateful the alliance may turn out to be to both parties, and however obvious its failure to the whole world—the stupid old thing blinks owlishly on at its own work, and professes itself totally unable to undo the knot which once it tied!

    * As suggested by Mrs. H. Ellis in her pamphlet A Noviciate
    for Marriage.

The only point where there is a permanent ground for State-interference—and where indeed there is no doubt that the public authority should in some way make itself felt—is in the matter of the children resulting from any alliance. Here the relation of the pair ceases to be private and becomes social; and the interests of the child itself, and of the nation whose future citizen the child is, have to be safe-guarded. Any contracts, or any proposals of divorce, before they could be sanctioned by the public authority, would have to contain satisfactory provisions for the care and maintenance of the children in such casualties as might ensue; nor ought there to be maintained any legal distinction between 'natural' and 'legitimate' children, since it is clear that whatever individuals or society at large may, in the former case, think of the conduct of the parents, no disability should on that account accrue to the child, nor should the parents (if identifiable) be able to escape their full responsibility for bringing it into the world.

If it be objected that such private contracts, or such facilitations of Divorce, as here spoken of, would simply lead to frivolous experimental relationships entered into and broken-off *ad infinitum*, it must be remembered that the responsibility for due rearing and maintenance of children must give serious pause to such a career; and that to suppose that any great mass of the people would find their good in a kind of matrimonial game of General Post is to suppose that the mass of the people have really never acquired or been taught the rudiments of common sense in such matters—is to suppose a case for which there would hardly be a parallel in the customs of any nation or tribe that we know of.

In conclusion, it is evident that no very great change for the better in marriage-relations can take place except as the accompaniment of deep-lying changes in Society at large; and that alterations in the Law alone will effect but a limited improvement. Indeed it is not very likely, as long as the present commercial order of society lasts, that the existing Marriage-laws—founded as they are on the idea of property—will be very radically altered, though they may be to some extent. More likely is it that, underneath the law, the common practice will slide forward into newer customs. With the rise of the new society, which is already outlining itself within the structure of the old, many of the difficulties and bugbears, that at present seem to stand in the way of a more healthy relation between the sexes, will of themselves disappear.

It must be acknowledged, however, that though a gradual broadening out and humanising of Law and Custom are quite necessary, it cannot fairly be charged against these ancient tyrants that they are responsible for all the troubles connected with sex. There are millions of people to-day who never could marry happily—however favorable the conditions might be—simply because their natures do not contain in sufficient strength the elements of loving surrender to another; and, as long as the human heart is what it is, there will be natural tragedies arising from the willingness or unwillingness of one person to release another when the former finds that his or her love is not returned.* While it is quite necessary that these natural tragedies should not be complicated and multiplied by needless legal interference—complicated into the numberless artificial tragedies which are so exasperating when represented on the stage or in romance, and so saddening when witnessed in real life—still we may acknowledge that, short of the millennium, they will always be with us, and that no institution of marriage alone, or absence of institution, will rid us of them. That entire and unswerving refusal to 'cage' another person, or to accept an affection not perfectly free and spontaneous, which will, we are fain to think, be always more and more the mark of human love, must inevitably bring its own price of mortal suffering with it; yet the Love so gained, whether in the individual or in society, will be found in the end to be worth the pang—and as far beyond the other love, as is the wild bird of Paradise that comes to feed out of our hands unbidden more lovely than the prisoner we shut with draggled wings behind the bars. Love is doubtless the last and most difficult lesson that humanity has to learn; in a sense it underlies all the others. Perhaps the time has come for the modern nations when, ceasing to be children, they may even try to learn it.

* Perhaps one of the most sombre and inscrutable of these natural tragedies lies, for Woman, in the fact that the man to whom she first surrenders her body often acquires for her (whatever his character may be) so profound and inalienable a claim upon her heart. While, either for man or woman, it is almost impossible to thoroughly understand their own nature, or that of others, till they have had sex-experience, it happens so that in the case of woman the experience which should thus give the power of choice is

frequently the very one which seals her destiny.
It reveals
to her, as at a glance, the tragedy of a lifetime which
lies before her, and yet which she cannot do other than
accept.

Made in the USA
Middletown, DE
07 April 2019